Leonard Stacy

A
Story of Bluegrass music

Acknowledgement:

This book is written in conjunction with my father, Leonard Stacy, to celebrate his life and his friendships with so many legendary bluegrass entertainers.

You will recognize some of the names, as they crossed over to country music, such as Ricky Skaggs and Keith Whitley and others.

This is a story of a life well lived and a man who was blessed with great friendships and a wonderful family.

This book is dedicated to my mother,
Mary Myrtle Miller Stacy,
Who is known to these legends of bluegrass as Myrt

And now as told by my Father
Leonard Stacy

Chapter 1
Growing up

I was born on a cold January day, the 25th of 1935 to be exact, and grew up on a hillside just above the dismal river in Buchanan County Virginia, in an old frame house that my daddy built out of slab boards from the local saw mill.

If you don't know what a slab board is, they're the skin of the trees that are shaved off to make the lumber, the left over pieces.

Back in those days a lot of folks built their places this way, I remember we had an old tin roof, but we didn't have a ceiling inside the old house; looking back I recall me and my brothers used to climb up into the rafters and play tag.

We'd also play tree tag, outside. Back there the trees grew real close together and we'd jump from limb to limb like monkeys and swing on grape vines playing tag. That must be why I liked to watch the show Tarzan in the sixties.

Every day we'd have to carry buckets down to the dismal river to fetch fresh water, and in the summer time that's where we'd go swimming.

There was a place in the river with a giant hole that they called hanging rock, because there was a giant rock that hung out over the river like a cliff, that's where we'd all, go.

We raised corn, and we had an old milking cow we'd have to chase every evening to milk her. We didn't have a field for her to graze in, so she just wondered around the mountain side all day and at night we'd listen for the sounds of the cow bell that hung around her neck and that's how we'd find her.

My mom cooked our meals on an old wood burning stove, we always had pinto beans and corn bread every evening and she would get up early in the morning every day and make us biscuits and gravy and sometimes we'd have corn meal gravy, she was a real good cook, she also like to spend her extra time sewing quilts.

Mom was born Lavicey Honaker, her dad was Tom Honaker and her momma died when she was little, all she remembered about her is she was full blooded Cherokee.

Her Pa married several more times and had a bunch of kids, that mom helped raise until she married.
Page 6

I can still remember walking down out off the hill in the mornings to catch the school bus, that took us to Patterson school, just up the river from where we lived. I was the oldest, of all boys and by the time I was grown, mom had 11 children, two that died early and the last one born was my sister Lindy.

Dad ran the local golf course, and was known to most folks as Shanghi, his real name was Ingram Stacy and he ran the local golf course.

The Story goes, back in the day they used to fly small planes over the golf course and drop chickens out, for the fun of it and then those on the ground tried to catch the chickens, well dad caught a Shanghi rooster and from then on that's what they called him.

When I was a kid dad had a moon shine steel and he was known for drinking and riding his old horse around singing.

The problem was he liked to shoot the water buckets off the neighbors' wells, while he was riding around and so when folks heard him singing, they'd go out and lower their water buckets down into their wells to keep him from putting holes in them.

My dad was a good singer and he loved Hank
Williams and Bill Monroe, I can still remember
that he'd get us kids and sit us down on the
porch of the old house and teach us to sing
songs like amazing grace and mansion on the
hill.

That's one of the first remembrances I have of
music. My dad was always singing around the
house, and we listened to the Grand Old Opry
on the radio every Saturday night when we
could get it.

Sometimes we'd have to put the batteries from
the radio into the oven and bake them to get
more juice and make them last longer. Back in
those days the batteries for the radio were about
a foot and a half long.

It was the early days of the Ryman Auditorium
and a man by the name of Bill Monroe made his
debut playing something different from country
music, they called it bluegrass. They were
originally known as the Monroe Brothers.

Bill Monroe was my dad's favorite singer and he
was playing a new kind of music, songs like
Blue Moon of Kentucky and Mule Skinner Blues.

When I was still a boy my dad quit drinking and started going to church, so from then on we all went to church at the Church of Christ in Deel Virginia, dads buried there in that cemetery.

My dad never owned a car so a friend of dad's would come by and pick us up on Sunday mornings; his name was McKinnely Matney; He was the local mail man.

When I was around 10 or 11 years old we moved to another place up off the hard top road called Janie Oakwood, above the Lavicey river; close to Grundy, where I went to school at Garden Creek High School.

We moved up into a holler behind the rail road tracks up behind my aunt Clementine's house, she was dad's sister. My grandpa James Stacy lived just down below us, we could see his house from up on the hill where we lived.

I remember one time when I was a teenager I'd been over in West Virginia, back then I had an old 1947 Ford Coupe; I paid $800.00 for it. and I got drunk with some old boys I know and when I drove back home I parked down below in my Grandpa's yard.

It was winter time with a snow on and cold outside, sometime in the night my grandpa came out there and got me and brought me into the house to sleep, otherwise I probably would've froze to death.

Another time I remember my dad took my car keys away from me so I hot wired that old coupe and broke the lock on the steering wheel and me and some old boys drove over to Bradshaw West Virginia and went drinking.

On the way back home coming down off the mountain I hit a stiff curve and the steering wheel locked up and over the mountain side we went. They claim it was so far down they didn't have enough cable to get down there and pull my car out, so they had to drive up the creek to get it.

Luckily no one got killed, it rolled several times on the way down, it's a wonder we all survived. Me and old Arnold Massey, Luther Dales and Ralph Matney and Charlie Rains were together that night.

We all crawled back up the mountain side to the road, and I remember old Luther got mad because he lost his shoes, somebody came a long and picked us up and took us to get help.
Page 10

My dad owned a coal mine and when I was about eleven years old; I'd go down and work with him in it.

I'd get so dirty with that black coal that when the day was done and I'd have to walk home, I'd walk along the railroad tracks back to the house; I didn't walk the road because I didn't want anyone to see me all dirty.

Back in those days they'd take a truckload of slate up to the top of the mountain and drop it down into a holler and we'd go and pick the lumps of coal out and we'd stack it in a sled and the horse would drag it down the hill and dad would sell the coal beside the road.

In those days, Grundy was a big town, every body went there on the weekends to shop and go to the movies, my dad liked to sit on the bench at the courthouse and watch people walking by.

The town had three Theatres', The Lynwood, The Alamo and The Morgan Theatre, where Bluegrass bands like the Monroe Brothers and the Stanley Brothers and others played there on a regular basis.

Page 11

So I recall when I was about twelve or thirteen years old, my daddy would let me work as a caddy at the golf course and I'd earned a nickel a hole, so if they played 18 holes, I got 18 nickels plus tips.

I'd save my money to pay for movies and music shows, back then it was .35 cents to get into see a double feature movie and the music show, it would have been around 1948. That's how I discovered the Stanley Brothers, Carter and Ralph.

You could sit on the front porch of the old house my dad built and see the highway down below and when I'd see that old car with the bass strapped to the roof, I knew the Stanley Brothers were playing, so I'd hitch hike into town for the show.

They were just starting out and making a name for themselves; They were in their mid twenties and I was barely a teenager. Ralph had just come home from the army and started playing Banjo with his brother Carter, who'd been playing lead with the Monroe Brothers.

The Monroe Brothers were from Kentucky, but the Stanley brothers, they were from the Clinch Mountains of Virginia, just over the mountains from where I grew up.

I'd watch them play their music; afterwards I'd strike up a conversation with them, I'd Talk to Carter but Ralph was bashful and he didn't have much to say and after awhile they remembered me when I came to their shows.

I loved this new kind of music and I watched how they played their instruments and I studied their perfection, I picked out that high tenor in Ralph's harmony and I loved that high lonesome sound.

So this was what I did most every weekend there was always someone playing bluegrass at the Morgan Theatre every week in Grundy, I got to know Bill Monroe pretty good also.

When I was around sixteen or seventeen I left Grundy with a friend of mine Millard Smith, he was nick named Trim Up, because he was over six foot tall, folks claimed when he was born he weighed two pounds and you could put him in a shoe box.

Page 13

We went up to Arlington Virginia where I went to work at Links food shop on Columbia Pike over by the Navy annex, I was flipping burgers to make a living. I would walk through the Arlington cemetery every day to get to work.

When I saved enough money I bought me a 1947 Hudson that I drove around until I threw a rod in it and I just left it beside the road.

After working there for awhile, me and an old boy named Emery Miller decided to join the marines, but when we went to sign up, we went into the wrong room and ended up in the Air force instead.

I was seventeen and I had to fake my Birth certificate, so I changed the date from 1935 to 1934 that made me 18 and legal.

I went to basic training in Sampson AFB in New York and when I finished they gave me a stripe for graduating, I was an Airman third class.

That's when I saw my cousin Mason Viers, he was in the Air force too and he was outside marching with a bunch of recruits, so I went over to look closer and make sure it was Mason. Sure enough it was.

Well I had a stripe and he didn't so I went over to his squadron leader and told him I wanted that man to help me pick up trash on the base, back then if you had a stripe you out ranked the newbie's, so me and Mason rented a bicycle and rode downtown. We went around to different beer joints and had fun

I lost contact with Mason and Emery Miller, we all got separated after that and I got sent to Hutchison Kansas, I went in to be in the motor pool but they gave me a 45 pistol and put me on the gate, I was classified as AP Military Police.

Well I got in trouble one night, I was on Guard duty and they had those big Jack Rabbits out there and I saw one jumping around in the bushes, so I decided to shoot the darn thing, problem was they knew how many bullets they gave me and at the end of my duty I was one bullet short, so they restricted me to the base for awhile.

Then there was this actress Ann Harding that used to come out to the base and pick up some of us boys and take us into town. She was beautiful and fun to be with

She drove a big old green Buick; she'd buy us drinks at the local beer joints. She came out and picked me up a few times, she was a little older than I was.

She'd come by often and she'd pick up a different soldier each time, some times she'd take a few of us into town. I didn't really know who she was until after I got out of the military and I saw her in some movies.

While I was in Hutchison my squadron officer came and got me one day and made me sit down and write a letter to my dad.

I guess I forgot to tell him I joined the military and somehow he got a hold of them and they made me write him and let him know I was okay and where I was.

I never did go over seas and it was during peacetime, so I did my time and sent money home to mom, I knew she needed help feeding the kids; dad broke his legs and couldn't work anymore.

I returned back to Garden Creek in April 1956, I was 20 years old.

Chapter 2

Me and Myrtle

It wasn't very long after I got home, that me and some old boys I knew, Arnold and Charlie, rode over to the Whitewood school house in my old 1948 Mercury.

One of those boys liked a girl that went to that school. It was an old two story red brick building sitting along side the road across from a little old creek.

We were hanging around outside, when some of the girls in the classroom upstairs started throwing notes out of the window to us down below. I caught Myrtles note.

After school let out me and the boys would follow the girls down the road on their way home talking to them, this went on for awhile.

My eye was on Myrtle and one day I followed her all the way past the old post office in Pilgrims Knob and up into the holler where she lived.

Her momma was Gertie Miller, a good Christian woman and when ever I'd come to call on Myrtle, she'd fix me some beans and cornbread, but her daddy Ulis, he didn't like me coming around and he said so, so I tried to avoid seeing him as much as possible.

I also remember Myrtle's Grandma Iola, she was Ulis's mother, and she lived down by the school house, along side that old creek, down in the bottom there across from the post office.

Well Iola she'd make me apple pies and Gertie she'd take an egg out of her hen house and go down to the store at the bottom of the hill and trade it for a pack of cigarettes for me. The Ladies liked me.

Myrtle would slip out of her bedroom window at night and meet me at the bottom of that hill and off we'd go. We slipped away every chance we got.

After awhile I took Myrtle to the Morgan Theatre down in Grundy, to see the Stanley Brothers. Since I'd been in the air force I hadn't seen any of their shows in years, but they remembered me when we went that night.

Over the next few months, we'd go watch them play music and one of those times we brought Myrtle's sister Edith Mae with us, and pretty soon she was dating Ralph, They dated for a long time as I recall.

It was during that time The Stanley Brothers were recording live shows with songs like Little Birdie, Dickenson County Breakdown, Thinking of the old Days, a song Carter wrote and You better get Right, along with Katie Hill, Wildwood Flower and Cumberland Gap.

Carter played the guitar and sang lead, Ralph was on the banjo singing high tenor, with Curley Lambert on the mandolin, Chubby Anthony on fiddle and Lindy Clear on Bass, the old Morgan Theatre was packed when ever they came to town.

Me and Myrtle were seeing each other steady over the next few months and I went to work in the Coal Mines, with Myrtle's brother Herman, everyone called him blue.

I didn't like working in those deep dark mines, I didn't like getting dirty, I didn't like climbing down into those dark caves.

A friend of mine from school Jackie Abbott, his dad owned a coal mine trucking company so I got a job with him driving a coal truck for awhile.

Old Jack Abbott and me became good life long friends and he eventually moved down to Florida close to where we moved to.

It was the spring of 1957 my uncle Larry came in to visit family, he asked me if I wanted to come to work for him. At the time he was one of the biggest painting contractors in the state of Florida, he was one of my mom's brothers.

So that's how I ended up in Florida; Me and Frog Ward, Myrtle's cousin, hitch hiked all the way leaving Myrtle behind.

The last feller that gave us a ride dropped us off in Largo, we were going to St Petersburg, and so we needed another ride to get there.

I called up my uncle Larry on the pay phone to see where he lived, then he asked me where we were, so I told him and he laughed and said, "well I'll just turn on my porch light, if you turn around you'll see my house" we were standing in front of his house, funny how that turned out.
Page 20

When we got down there we lived on oranges
for a couple of weeks, until we got paid, because
we didn't have any money

So we stayed with my Uncle Larry and his wife
Martha, after about a month when I'd made
enough money, me and Frog Hitch Hiked back
to Virginia

I went to see Myrtle and we ended up riding a
grey hound bus back to St Petersburg together,
where we stayed with my Uncle Larry and his
wife Martha again, saving money to get our own
place.

Myrtle was sixteen at the time and her mommy
and daddy called the law and reported her as a
runaway.

When my Aunt Martha got wind of the situation
she called the law and turned Myrtle in. They
picked her up and put her on a bus back to
Virginia.

Now the Law was looking for me for taking her
across state lines, so I left Larry's house and
went to stay with my Uncle Kernel and his wife
Mary a few miles away.

My uncle Kernel kept hiding me from the law, one time in the middle of the night I had to crawl up into the loft to hide from them.

I decided to go back to Virginia so late one night Kernel drove me out of St Petersburg and dropped me off on highway 19 and I hitch hiked back.

When I got there, the law found me and put me in the Grundy County Jail, then they sent me to bland county farm in Clintwood for my sentence, but by then I didn't have enough time left so they wouldn't keep me and they turned me loose.

Me and Myrtle got married and had a little girl we named Bonnie Mae in August 1957, We soon left Virginia and went to Flint Michigan to find work and we stayed with Myrtle's brother Alfred and his wife Dorothy.

I had a 1953 Pontiac and we drove up there with snow on the ground, with no heater in the car, we about froze to death. But we made it up there.

It was so cold up there we couldn't stand it, so we headed back to Virginia where we stayed for a short time and our second child Carol was born that September 1960, we named her Vicey Carol after my mom, the winter was coming so we decided to go back to Florida.

I was working with the painters union and we were living in St Petersburg and in October 1961 our 3rd daughter Donna was born, we were living off of 49th street, I was working out of town, when I come home Myrtle said I got a surprise for you, here's Donna.

We moved around a lot, staying with family, finding our own place and trying to make ends meet, we stayed in the Largo and Saint Petersburg area going back to Virginia often to see family and in April 1963 our 4th child, a son Leonard David was born.

At some time or another we moved to Arlington Virginia for awhile but after a cold winter up there, we went back to Florida.

We stayed with friends we'd met before when we lived in that area for a few months while I found another job.

I heard about a house for sale across the Causeway Bridge in Tampa, so I pawned my shot gun for the dawn payment and bought it.

Myrtle and the kids were happy when we moved into the house on Jean Street. In April of 1969 we had are 5th child, Jeffery, who was to be the youngest of five.

It was in this house on Jean street that me and Myrtle raised our kids for about twenty years, always traveling back and forth to see the family in Virginia.

After we moved back down to Florida, me and Myrtle started going to bluegrass shows and we'd see Ralph and Carter, Bill Monroe, Jim and Jesse, Jimmy Martin all the greats of the time. Whenever Ralph saw me in the audience he would send me out a song from the stage.

Unknown to me at the time, shortly after me and Myrtle moved back to Florida, Carter and Ralph Stanley moved to Live oak Florida, just a couple hours north of where we were living.

Carter and Ralph Stanley had a TV show that aired in Tampa on TV 13 called the Jim Walters Jamboree.

Ralph always joked with me and told me he followed me down to Florida, and so my friendship with Ralph and Carter continued into and through the sixties.

Chapter 3

The Stanley Brothers
Liveoak Florida- Years 1958 - 1966

The Stanley Brothers got an opportunity to host their own TV show, it was called The Jim Walters Jamboree, broadcasting from Live Oak, Florida, near the Suwannee River.

The show was seen all over the state of Florida and I tuned in every week to watch, that how I found out they were living down here.

During this time Carter met him a girl named Mary and they got married and had children, Carter, Bill, Bobby, Doris and Jeannie, all of whom still live in the Live Oak or the surrounding area.

As it was Lawtey Florida put on big Bluegrass shows twice a year and we went up and saw The Stanley Brothers play music twice a year and we caught their shows up in Virginia from time to time, when we'd go home to visit.

In those days the Stanley Brothers were putting out some of the best music I'd ever heard, with songs like Old Country Church,
Who will sing for me, working on a Building, Memories of Mother, Harbor of Love, I'll Fly Away and Little Bessie, on their 1963 album "Old Country Church".

They were playing songs like, In the Pines, on shows like Reno & Smiley; they were playing shows and putting out a new album every year.

Like I said before me and Myrtle went back and forth to Virginia to see the folks several times a year and I guess the last time I saw the Stanley brothers together was at the Richland's drive in theater, I'm thinking it was 4th of July weekend in 1966.

They were standing up on the roof of the building that the projector was in and did the show from up there, back in those days they didn't always have a stage.

Jim and Jesse also played that show and I remember I'd been talking with them back stage and asked if they'd play a song for mom, she was with us at the show, she was a big fan of theirs and they did, it made her real happy.

The Stanley Brothers played all kinds of events, from festivals, to theatres, school houses, bars, and drive in movie theatres, just about anywhere that they could get booked and so my friendship continued with Carter and Ralph.

On Dec 1, 1966 carter passed away, Ralph wasn't sure if he wanted to continue with the music, he finally decided to go on, putting Larry Sparks (at one time it was a rumor that Larry belonged to Carter) as lead singer to his high Tenor.

In Memory of Carter, Ralph Wrote and recorded the song, Let me rest (on a peaceful mountain), one of my favorites to this day.

Returning to Smith Ridge, Ralph started a yearly festival in Memory of Carter called Carter Stanley Memorial festival, years later after a family lawsuit the name was changed to the Hills of Home Bluegrass Festival.

I should mention that when I retired in the eighties, I moved to North Florida, to a small town called Branford by the Suwannee River, and close to Live Oak, where Carters kids were raised.

Over the years I got to know Bill and Carter and Jeannie pretty good, I'd see them at Ralph's Hills of Home Festival every year, and Jeannie and my daughter played some music together for a short time.

Ralph invited Jeannie to sing on one of his Cd's, so me and Myrtle drove her up to Virginia to the recording studio. I've kept in touch with Carters kids over the years and they call and check on me from time to time.

Chapter 4
Dr Ralph Stanley
& The Clinch Mountain Boys

In the 70's Ralph Stanley and the Clinch Mountain Boys traveled the Bluegrass circuit across the United States from Virginia to California , from Florida to New York.

The first band members after Carter were Larry Sparks on lead guitar and Lead Singer, George Shuffler on Bass, Chubby Anthony on Fiddle, later on Ralph hired Roy Lee Centers, some people say he was the best next to Carter. He was murdered in 1974.

Later in the mid 70's, Band members included, Curly Ray Cline on Fiddle, Jack Cooke on Bass, Keith Whitley as lead singer, Ricky Skaggs on Mandolin, he also had other lead singers that included Charlie Sizemore for many years, Sammy Adkins, and Ernie Thacker, just to name a few.

Myrtle and me went to see Ralph every time he came to Florida, and sometimes when Ralph had extra time, he'd stay over an extra few days and we'd go deep sea fishing.

We also traveled back and forth to Virginia
several times a year to see the family, and I
always included a memorial weekend trip so I
could go to Ralph's Festival up on smith's ridge
in Coeburn.

In the mid 70's Ralph and Jimmi came down and
vacationed at our house on Jean street in Tampa,
they brought their girls with them Lisa and
Tonya, Ralph two hadn't been born yet.

Ralph had a show at the Armory in Tampa and
Keith Whitley and Ricky Skaggs were playing in
the band at the time, they stayed over night at
our house, then those two went on over to
Daytona Beach for the rest of the week.

Ralph and Jimmi stayed at my house and we
went deep sea fishing several times and went
swimming out on the Courtney Campbell
Causeway.

I guess you could say I've always been
mischievous, and I always had fun ducking
everyone in the water when we'd go swimming.

I remember chasing Ralph a few times on the
beach, trying to get him and he would run from
me because he was afraid of the water, we had
some good fun times.

Page 31

One time I took Ralph over to a jam session in Tampa at Tommy Perkins place and they were all surprised to see me and Ralph show up.

They were playing one of Ralphs songs and when we walked in, they all stopped playing, they were surprised to see Ralph Standing their in person. Boy he got a kick out of that.

The next time I was there they'd painted foot steps on the floor where Ralph had walked, with a sign that said Ralph Stanley walked here.

I also took Ralph over to the Bluegrass parlor to meet Tom Henderson and Jim Johnson, who had a radio program in Tampa called this is Bluegrass.

Ralph was interviewed on the air, The Bluegrass parlor was a music store that Tom Henderson owned and he had a band from there called the Bluegrass Parlor band.

While visiting with us, Ralphs old bus broke down while he was here, the transmission went out on it. So he had to go back with someone else and get the bus fixed before they could drive it back up.

Page 32

Sometimes Ralph would stay with me and Myrtle a few days, sometimes he'd stay a week, sometimes he brought his wife Jimmi.

During Labor Day weekend, Sept of 1978 we were in Virginia at a show and we stopped by Ralph and Jimmi's house over in Coeburn to see the new baby, Ralph Stanley II was just a few weeks old.

Ralph was out on the road but we got to spend some time with Jimmi.

Chapter 5
Ricky Skaggs and Keith Whitley

I was at the festival where Ralph first heard Ricky Skaggs and Keith Whitley play music. Ralph was late for the show and the MC said we're going to bring on these two young boys who are going to do some Stanley Brothers singing.

Ralph had a flat tire that caused the band to be late, and when they drove up, they heard their music playing; Ricky and Keith were still on stage singing. Ralph told me, he thought they were playing their records, because it sounded like him and Carter.

And so Ralph hired both of them and they became part of the Clinch Mountain Boys story. Back in those days I liked to have myself a beer or two and I remember giving those two a beer from time to time.

Me and Myrtle traveled with a camper back in those days to festivals all over the south east United states, we'd follow the music to Virginia, Kentucky, North Carolina, South Carolina, Georgia, Tennessee, Florida we were gone most every weekend to a show.

My youngest son Jeff said Keith taught him how
to dip snuff, and would let him sneak and have a
beer; he was about 10 or 11 years old at the time.

Ralph told me one time he was in Kenton Texas
and Keith got drunk and was raising hell on the
bus and Ralph got mad because he wouldn't
shut up so he stopped the bus and made him get
off and left him on the side of the road.

Ralph said Keith got back to the Hardees
restaurant in Coeburn before they did. He
hitchhiked all the way home, or so he said.

Years later I saw Keith after he hit the big time in
Tampa, he was doing a show, and after the
concert he was signing autographs and me and
my Daughter Donna were standing off to the
side waiting for him to finish.

At some point he looked up and said hey
Leonard, give me a few more minutes and we'll
walk back stage and talk.

I was surprised that Keith remembered me, I
wasn't sure if he would, I was going to remind
him where I knew him from, he was just a kid
when I knew him and a lot of years had gone by
since then.

Page 35

We went back stage and talked for awhile, then Keith lit a cigarette, I took it away from him and reminded him, he'd told me a long time ago, when he had his first number one hit, he'd quit smoking, Keith laughed and agreed, he remembered, and said he'd work on quitting.

We came back the next day for the second show and Keith was worried about his bus, it broke down and he was saying he couldn't wait to get back to Nashville to see Lorrie (Lorrie Morgan) his wife, she was leaving on tour with her first big hit, Dear Me, and he wanted to get home, so he was going to fly. That was the last time I saw him alive.

Ricky, I'd see him a few times over the years when he'd come in and do a show at Ralph's Hills of Home Festival in Virginia, one time Ralph had me pick him up at the airport in Bristol Johnson City.

Last time I saw Ricky was back stage at the 50th Hills of Home Bluegrass Festival that Ralph II put on, Memorial Day Weekend 2022.

Me and my daughter Donna were back stage sitting with Jimmi Stanley most of the weekend and when Ricky came up to the stage to do his show, he sat back stage and visited with us.
Page 36

He was very friendly and he talked to us while he tuned his mandolin and told us how he managed to get and restore Peewee's original mandolin, then he asked Donna to hold it for him while he tuned another mandolin.

We all took pictures and some video, he put on a real good show and he had a big crowd. The Stanley Family gifted him with a legacy award; he was the 4th recipient to receive it.

Chapter 6
Dr Ralph Stanley
A friendship continues

Sometime along the way, I started helping Ralph out with things he needed done at the festival and around his house. I'd do a little painting at the old home place and his wife Jimmi, she had an old statue of a dog out there in the yard, she liked for me to paint every year.

Myrtle worked the Gate and helped sell his CD's, too. I'd show up a few days early and help get things ready for the festival, sometimes I'd get family members to come over and volunteer.

One year Myrtle and me and our daughter Donna went up a few days early and I painted the original old stage down at the bottom of the hill and Donna painted a picture of Ralph and Carter with some scenery on the back wall, years later Ralph II a picture down on the old stage and made it his CD cover.

Some people may not know it but when that first stage was built, people like Ricky Skaggs and Keith Whitley helped build it. Some folks laughed and say that's why it's leaning Ricky Helped build it.
Page 38

Years Later the new stage was built up on top of the hill and me and Donna painted it also. Since then some others have painted over it.

When they first opened the Ralph Stanley museum, I filmed Ralph walking around in there while he told me about all the stuff that was in there and then I donated the video to the Museum.

They gave me and Myrtle life time passes to the museum. It's a beautiful place with lots of memories for Ralph. Matter of fact we were there when Steve Sparkman got married at the museum.

Did I mention I've got video's of those bluegrass shows going back into the seventies.

I've been filming the festivals since they made video cameras so I've got just about everyone who was anyone on video.

I took hours of video's back stage and on the road with Ralph, I've even got the only video of Bill Monroe's funeral service taken inside the church, his son James Monroe, let me go inside and made everyone else stay outside.

While me and my daughter Donna were up at the 50th Hills of Home Festival, we went over to the museum and videoed me walking through it, telling some stories.

I guess I should mention Myrtle my wife passed away Jan 13 or 2021, so she wasn't able to be with me on this trip.

You can go on YouTube and see some of our videos from this trip. We also made a video of the Dr Ralph Stanley highway and the Carter Stanley Highway drive up to the festival. YouTube Channel is under Donna Stacy

Chapter 7
Traveling with Ralph on the Road

When I retired in 1989 Ralph asked me if I wanted to drive for him on some of his long trips, I remember the first one was up to Maine, and we were in that old MCI he had, Gary Brewer later on bought that bus from Ralph.

It was so cold we about froze to death, Hillard Blankenship his regular bus driver (They called him the duck, because he couldn't keep the bus straight on the highway, it would waddle back and forth while he was driving)
Well he said the heater was broken.

I was about to freeze to death and I was setting on the bus while they did their show so I decided to look at the heater and I managed to fix it, it just hadn't been turned on, everyone was glad to have heat going to the next show.

Every year Ralph would do a coast to coast trip out to California and back with show dates in between. He'd be gone for six or seven weeks, so I made these trips with him every year.

I remember one time we were in Berkley California and had some extra time so, me and E.C. decided to take a train ride to see some of the sights, well, we got on a train and ended up in a tunnel for 2 hours, when we got to the other side, we had to ride it back through the tunnel, we didn't get to see anything but darkness for 4 hours each way.

When we were in San Francisco we went to see Alcatraz, me and James Alan Shelton, James Price and Miles Ward, we went over by boat, for a day trip. I saw the Pacific Ocean for the first time.

While we were in California, they gave Ralph and all of us a place to stay in a big old mansion at Pebble beach golf course.

We went up and down the California coast line doing different shows, Jim Lauderdale was usually on tour with Ralph on the west coast tours, Ralph and Jim recorded an album while out there, titled I Feel like singing today.

I remember one time in Arizona, we left flagstaff right after a show and had to go to Tuscan Arizona, and Ralph told me to find the shortest route on the map, so I did.

Four hours later we come up to a mountain, with the road blocked off, too much snow on top, so they wouldn't let us cross, I asked the state trooper how to get to Tuscan and he said, go back to flagstaff and go back to interstate, it ended up being the long way around. But we made it to Tuscan in time to do the show.

Over the years I drove Ralph Stanley and the Clinch Mountain Boys from Virginia to Ohio, California, Poplar Gap, New Mexico, Arizona, Colorado, Missouri, Kansas, Oklahoma, Maine, Kentucky, Tennessee and New York, including places in between

Most people don't know but Ralph was a jokester, if you got to know him you'd find he had a fun personality, he liked to pull jokes on everyone on the bus.

For example he told stories about me like I'd go crazy if I didn't get my medicine and I said I murdered my brother in law.

I remember one time that Ralph two gave Curly Ray some X-lax and he had to sit on a bucket all the way to the next show.

I bet Two remembers that, old Curly kept saying it must've been those green apples he picked and ate along the way.

I remember one time the air conditioner went out on the bus, I don't remember where we were, but me and old Ernie Thacker slept outside on an old hay wagon.

Sometime in the nineties Ralph recorded a song me and my brother in law Alfred Miller wrote called Little Jimmy.

Along the way Ralph wanted to honor the ones who had contributed to his career and music so he started a tradition of giving away a Carter Stanley Memorial Guitar.

These were special made guitars from out of California made exclusively for Dr Ralph with detailed inlays of silver and designs like white doves. They made only 58 of the Carter Stanley guitars with Ralph's signature inside.

Over the years people like Charlie Sizemore and Ricky Skaggs were honored to be the recipient of this one of a kind guitar.

I was sure surprised and never expected it but one year Ralph Called me up on the stage and gave me one of them, it is beautiful with silver inlays with white doves on the neck, it is my prized possession.

Let me tell you how that day happened. I was at the Hills of Home festival on Memorial Day weekend like I always am, never missed one and I was down on the front row video taping.

Jeannie's Stanley's husband Davey came and got me and said Ralph wanted me to introduce Big Jim Williams who was getting the guitar that year.

Big Jim Williams played mandolin on the movie of "Oh Brother where art thou" and I used to introduce him every year at the Sullivan Family's Music show, Margie and Enoch, it was held in Nashville at the Ernest Tubb Record shop the first Friday in November, so we knew each other pretty well I'd say.

So I went on back stage and when it was time I introduced Big Jim and he went out on the stage and got his guitar and said a few words.

Page 45

Just as he was leaving the stage Ralph called me out there and said "Come on out here Leonard I got something for you" so I walked out and he said "I got this here guitar for you if you want it" he joked.

I said "Sure I want it "then he asked me if I'm gonna learn to play it and I said "I'll try." I was surprised and that's a day I'll never forget.

Ralph and me were friends all of our lives by that time he was up in his seventies and I was in my sixties, I guess he wanted to honor me for driving his bus and promoting his music on my bluegrass Radio Programs.

He told me later I had made lots of contribution to the music.

Chapter 8
Ralph inducted into the Hall of Fame

In 1992 Ralph Stanley was inducted into the
Country Music Hall of Fame, me and Myrtle and
our daughter Donna went to the event in
Nashville with Ralph and his family, his wife
Jimmi, daughters Lisa, Tonya and Ralph II.

There were lots of recording artist there like,
Allison Krauss, I remember, Bob Dylan, at that
time Ralph was filming his life story called
down from the mountain and Ralph had a
camera crew following him around.

He told my daughter to stay close at the event he
would make her famous, we didn't know what
he meant but at some point in the evening he
came over to our dinner table with the camera
man and said hello to us.

Later on we found out we were in his movie
about his life, if you get a chance to see it,
"Down from the mountain" the Story of Ralph
Stanley.

We used to get invited to events like that by
Ralph, another time when they first reopened
the Ryman auditorium; Ralph invited us to come
up for the show. We got to be back stage and Bill
Monroe was playing also.

While we were in Ralphs dressing room, Porter
Wagoner stopped by to say hello to Ralph, My
daughter got her picture taken with him.

We were there all day watching them rehearse
and setting up equipment, my daughter tells the
story, she was standing on the stage earlier in
the day just looking around from the point of
view of so many famous singers, and she started
singing sweet dream by Patsy Cline and Bill
Monroe walked up behind her and said he come
looking cause he thought he heard Patsy singing.

Another time Ralph was playing at Patty
Loveless Homecoming show in Elkhorn
Kentucky, and we got invited to go and meet
Patty Loveless, Vince Gill, Bobby Bare.

Chapter 9

The Suwannee Valley Bluegrass Show & The Bluegrass Express

As the years rolled by more and more, we went to these events, like Ralph's Birthday celebration he started holding.

It was during these years I started my radio Program Suwannee Valley Bluegrass Show out of Chiefland Florida.

My daughter Donna was working at our local radio station and when the GM retired she left Donna to manage the station, so I approached Donna with my idea about a bluegrass radio program and that's how it was born.

We played a one hour program on Sunday mornings and the show became a huge success. I worked with a man by the name of Jerry Trail, he ran the board and talked with me live as we played the music and so began our friendship.

After several years on the air, at 97.3 FM WLQH Chiefland, the station owner decided to sell out to a larger radio station and so that ended our radio show, but that wasn't the end.

The Suwannee Valley Bluegrass Hour became the Suwannee Valley Music show on 101.7 FM WDJY Trenton, my good friend Jerry Trail was on air on Saturday mornings with his program and was known as the Trail Boss, along with Lynwood Koonce at the sharecropper, well they brought me into the stations and we talked on the air and the next thing I know I got my radio program going again on a new station.

We ran for many years as the Suwannee Valley Bluegrass show and hosted several bluegrass festivals in the area, Ralph came down and performed at one of them, we hosted smaller festivals with some local bluegrass bands also.

Later on that station was also sold and became a satellite office for a larger radio group and I found my self with Jerry Trail, the old Trail Boss working out of Lake City Florida on a much larger radio station 102.7 FM that covered most of north central Florida.

Together we hosted a very popular radio program called the Bluegrass Express every Sunday from five to nine will live call in request and over the years with all my traveling with Ralph I had made a lot of friends in the music business.

Entertainers from all over would send me their latest CD so I could play it on the air and I got their phone numbers and I'd call them and talk to them over the air.

Ralph Stanley would call, Jim Lauderdale, Gary Brewer, Larry Sparks, JD Crowe, Raymond Fairchild, Little Roy Lewis, Larry Gillis, Rhonda Vincent, and the list goes on.

 The Bluegrass Express was one of the highest rated and most popular weekend broadcast in North Florida.

We promoted every festival we could and even had the promoters call in and talk about their festival, from Withlacoochee, Yee haw Junction, Roadeavers boys ranch with Norman Adams, to Ralphs Annual Hills of Home, to the Lewis Family festival.

Page 51

The Bluegrass Express was on air for close to a decade, all in all I spent about twenty years on the radio promoting Bluegrass Gospel Music with my friends both the entertainers and the festival promoters and I made a lot of fans along the way.

Seems like where ever I go people know who I am and when I talk they recognize me.

Chapter 10
The Cumberland Highlanders

Me and Myrtle traveled all over to bluegrass festivals over the years, we started going to a new festival up at Jerusalem Ridge in Kentucky where Bill Monroe was from.

A man by the name of Campbell Mercer started a show up there calling it the Cumberland Highlanders show; he filmed it and it aired on the RFD Channel.

Well I knew a lot of the entertainers and had done some MC work on and off from time to time, with different festivals , so the next thing I know old Campbell had me out there bringing on some of the Entertainers

His show was popular and we went every year and I'd watch it on the RFD channel every week. Family and friends would call me and tell me they saw me and Myrtle on TV, Myrt would sit on the stage with a few others.

Old Campbell had some big names on his festival like Dr Ralph Stanley and the Clinch Mountain Boys, Joe Isaac and his wife Stacy were regulars and old Lynwood Lunsford played banjo, I knew him from when he played with Jimmy Martin back in the nineties.

After some very successful years the Jerusalem Ridge festival was shut down by local authorities based on law suits and permits, I never did know the whole story and Campbell Mercer was never been able to reach since then.

Which is very unfortunate as the festival and TV program were much loved and enjoyed by many.

Chapter 11
Jim Lauderdale

Some of the Entertainers I've met over the years have become good friends and I try to catch their music show when ever I can.

Jim Lauderdale is one of those people, this man travels the world and plays his music and when he is close to my home I go to see him, he comes to Florida two or three times a year and I'll catch him at Ralphs Festival every year.

For those of you who don't know him, he's one of the nicest people I've ever met and probably one of the best song writers there ever was. He recorded with Ralph Stanley the CD titled, "I Feel like singing today"

The first time I met Jim was when I was driving the bus for Ralph on tour out in California. I think the first show he did was Freight and Salvage in Berkley California.

Jim never did ride the bus with us, in between shows but he always showed up the next day for the show.

Some of you may not know, but Jim is one of the most well known songwriters in Nashville, he wrote hit songs for people like George Strait, Patty Loveless, Dixie Chicks, Blake Shelton and Vince Gill just to name a few.

Those hit songs include: "Half way down" and "You don't seem to miss me" for Patty Loveless, "The king of Broken Hearts" and "Where the sidewalk ends" both on George Straits Pure Country album, The Dixie Chicks song "Hole in my Head". And Mark Chestnuts hit: "Gonna get a life" just to name a few.

He also wrote and recorded an album with Ralph Stanley and the Clinch Mountain Boys called Lost in the Lonesome Pines, which won a Grammy award for the song "she's looking at me".

I video taped the recording sessions in California, and I also videoed all of us on the bus and the scenery and all the shows.
I've got a lot of videos from those days.

I remember during that recording session, Jim didn't want Jack Cooke to play bass, so he flew in George Shuffler from North Carolina to play the bass.

I remember when he first got there Ralph asked him, "how many songs do you have Jim", and he answered "well I got three, but I'll finish the rest of them as we go along", and he ended up with about 25, but they only put 12 on the CD.

Over time Jim and I became friends, he'd always show up every year on the California tour schedule and Ralph had him booked on his Hills of Home Festival every year after that.

Like I said I always tried to go see his show when he was playing close by.

One time I was headed over to his show in Jacksonville Florida and I got turned around and was running late.

Just so happened the show was the day before my birthday, and when I finally got there, I walked up to where they sell the tickets and told them my name to get my ticket and they said we've been waiting on you.

They took me back stage and Jim was already on stage and when I walked in, he had the whole audience stand up and sing happy birthday to me.

Page 57

Jim would always invite me back stage and I'd meet other entertainers, during this time I had my radio show, so a lot of them entertainers started giving me their CD's and I'd play them on the air, promoting their music.

Same with Ralph Stanley and every where I'd go, entertainers would give me their CD's.

Chapter 12
Bill Monroe
The Father of Bluegrass Music

The first time I met Bill was at the Morgan Theatre when I was a kid, and later when I got back from the Air force I'd see him and say hello. So over the years we also became friends I'd see him at the bluegrass festivals he'd always come over to talk to Ralph.

Bill was hard to get along with; if you drank a beer he wouldn't even talk to you, if he smelt beer on your breath he'd just walk away. He was a strong man; he could grab you with just one hand and jerk you down on his lap.

When bill got up there in years he'd kind of get a little confused from time to time, several times he tried to go home with me and Myrtle.

One time he tried to get in the car and leave with us and Myrt asked me "what would we do with him",

I said "treat him like anyone else I guess".

Bill always had his show at Bean Blossom in Indiana, for seven days in June, me and Myrtle traveled to this show every year, so we knew him pretty good.

He was my dad's favorite singer.

Last time I saw Bill was in the mid nineties at the Ryman Auditorium, He and Ralph were doing a show there. The Ryman had been closed down for repairs for a long time and it had just been reopened.

They put on a good show, it was televised on TV. Bill was up there in age and it was shortly before he passed away, when I spoke to him he was confused, but when he took the stage he was right on que with his playing and singing.

His voice was like no other and when him and Ralph sang together it was special to hear.

I didn't think about it or know that would be the last time I saw Bill Monroe, he was traveling with family members at the time, I think it was a special occasion that he came out to play.

When bill died I was the only one allowed in the church house to film his funeral, James Monroe gave me permission. I still got that video somewhere.

There were news media trucks from all over parked outside and entertainers everywhere at that little church house. It was a sad day.

Chapter 13
Entertainers I knew over the years

Well I got to meet and get to know many of the legends of Bluegrass; they all knew me as Leonard and my wife as Myrt, which is short for Myrtle. Ralph Stanley started calling her Myrt so everyone in Bluegrass called her Myrt also.

But I got to be friends with many legends of Bluegrass over the years; I'd play their music on my radio programs and see them out on the road with Ralph.

Entertainers like:

Larry Stephenson
Doyle Lawson & Quicksilver
Jim & Jesse The Virginia boys
Jimmy Martin-
The Lewis family- Little Roy
Sullivan Family – Margret and Enoch
Carl Story and wife Helen,-
– Gold Wing Express –
Jimmy Dailey-from Doyle Lawson
Little Jimmy Dickens
Jeff and Sherri Easter

Mac Wiseman
Jesse McReynolds
The Osborne brothers
Larry Sparks
Marty Raybon
Wade Mainer
Del McCoury
James King
Dave Evans
Larry Sparks
Reno & Smiley
Raymond Fairchild
JD Crowe
Melvin Goins
Kody Norris
Larry Gillis

And the list goes on, my apologies if I miss
someone's name

Chapter 14
Friends of Bluegrass

Along the way I got to meet entertainers from other music Genre's, performers who admired Ralph's Old time mountain style of music, many of who recorded with him over the years.

I sat in the studio many times watching the songs all come together, with singers like Patty Loveless, Joe Isaac, Jim Lauderdale, and met entertainers back stage like Vince Gill, Bob Dylan, Garth Brooks, Trisha Yearwood, Jimmy Deans, Porter Wagoner, Dwight Yoakam, Marty Raybon, The Isaacs, and so many more.

Over the years so many people kept the mountain style bluegrass music going and I'm glad I got to be a part of it. I hope it continues for a long time to come, long after I'm gone.

Some of those people who deserve credit for their part in Bluegrass music are the festival promoters.

People like Norman and Judy Adams who put together festivals for over 45 years, like the Cherokee Bluegrass Festival, and the New Years

Festival in Jekyll Island, the Palatka Bluegrass
Festival in Florida, the anual South Carolina
Bluegrass Festival in Myrtle Beach, SC

Promoters like Ken Clark who started the Lawty
Florida Festivals way back in the early days.

Doug and Alan Lanier: who put on a festival up
in Georgia, Rebecca Rose comes to mind, she
passed away early in life and was a beautiful
person and singer.

Jean and Bob Cornet from the Spirit of
Suwannee Music Park
Withlacoochee Bluegrass Festival
Yee Haw Junction
Otter Springs

I've been to so many festivals over the years I
can't remember them all

Chapter 15
A friendship comes to an end

It was a sad day when Ralph Died, June 23rd of 2016, me and Myrtle had just been up to his festival Memorial Day weekend. Ralph was too sick to attend that year and I didn't get to see him that time.

Several years before his passing when we'd go up we saw how he was getting more frailer every time. It wasn't a surprise when he passed away.

Myrtle and me went back up to Virginia for the funeral. A private service was held in the funeral home and then a public service was held on the stage at his festival grounds.

Patty Loveless and Vince Gill sang along with many of the Clinch Mountain Boys.

Ralph's coffin was placed on the stage in the same place where he'd stood so many times with the cinch mountain boys, singing his old time mountain music, playing his banjo claw hammer style, his voice singing that high tenor.

After the music was sung everyone followed the coffin up to the cemetery, walking behind as a man played the bag pipes.

He was buried next to his mom Lucy, Carter and his wife Mary in the family cemetery on the top of the mountain.

Me and Myrtle drove back to Florida with sadness in my heart, it's been six years since his passing and I'm proud to say I knew the man, his music lives on and Ralph II has done a good job performing at festivals and singing the songs of the Stanley Brothers and keeping his memory alive.

Chapter 16
The Rest of the story

Writing this book I've been able to go back over my life and relive those days, and enjoy those memories.

In the last six years I have continued to travel to the bluegrass festivals as best as I can. Myrtle passed away in 2021 and I turned 87 this past year, so I don't get around as good as I used to.

A lot of those entertainers I knew have passed away in these last years, I keep up with the ones still living and check on the widows of a few of them.

I talk to Jimmi Stanley often; we talk about Ralph and Myrtle and how much we miss them. Talk about the good old days we all had.

I talk to Carl Story's widow from time to time and Ray Franks widow Jean.

Jeanie Stanley and Bill Stanley call me often, Bill doesn't get out of the house anymore with his health issues, and Jeanie and Davey didn't get to go to the festival this last Memorial Day.

Page 68

Nathan Stanley, Ralph's grandson has done a couple of shows down here in Florida about an hour from me, so I've been over to see him. He also has a radio program On Monday nights at 7pm, I give him a listen every week.

Jim Lauderdale is still doing his shows down here twice a year at the spirit of Suwannee in Live Oak, so I've seen him recently.

Norman Adams turned over his festivals down here to Ernie Evans so I've made a few of those shows.

I'm keeping busy after recovering from a Heart attack and five strokes in early 2022, I just turned 87 and I'm doing good.

I'm working with my daughter Donna to take my video library, all those recordings I've made both on stage and off stage and put them in a format from VHS to digital and plan on uploading to You tube channel.

I've been told by many I should write a book, so here it is. Some stories can't be told and are private from on the road.

Hope you enjoy the story and the pictures.

I am Leonard Stacy, the Host of the Suwannee Valley Bluegrass show and the Bluegrass Express, also known as the Sheriff of Bluegrass to many.

I've enjoyed my life, loved my wife and kids and been blessed to grow up in those mountains and get to know the people I did.

If you reading this and knew me and I forgot to mention you, my apologies, I did my best to include everyone.

Leonard Stacy on the radio

Ralph Stanley
giving me the Carter Stanley Memorial
guitar

Me and Little Roy Lewis
with Myrtle and kids

Myrtle and me in the early years

Myrtle in front of an old Cadillac I had

Me and Myrtle at Ralphs Festival

Back stage with Ralph and his family at
the Opry

Ralph and Jimmi and me back stage

Me, Donna, Ralph II and David

Me and Myrtle

At Ralphs Birthday Party

Me and Myrtle when we first met

My Air force Picture I was 17 years old

Me and Myrtle 1956

Our kids,
Bonnie, Vicey Carol, Donna, David &
Jeffery, me in the back ground

Bill Monroe
in the early years with David

Me with Larry Sparks and David

Me and David with Melvin Goins

Me with Rhonda Vincent

Me with Ricky Skaggs

Me picking on an old Guitar

Jack Cooke
Bass player for Ralph Stanley

Gold Wing Express

Little Roy Lewis

Gary Brewers Bus

Me and Myrtle in the early years

Me and mom and brothers and sister

Me and Brothers and sister later in life

My old home place Garden Creek , VA

Me and Myrtle
when we first moved to Florida

My Mom - LaVicey Honacker Stacy

Myrtle's home place over
in
Pilgrims Knob VA

Ralphs first tour bus back in the 70's

Myrt with mom and the kids

Me up in Pilgrims Knob 2013

Me and my daughter Donna
in the recording studio

visiting my dad's grave

My Grandparents
James Stacy and wife Nancy Dawson

In pilgrims knob at Gertie and Ulis house
with my great grandson Matthew Larson

Myrtle picking apples off the tree

My dad Ingrim Stacy

Myrtle and my mom back in 1957

Gertie Miller

Our Children
Bonnie, Carol, (baby- Jeffery)
Donna & David

Myrtle and me
enjoying our Golden years

This book was written for my dad and mom, to celebrate their life together as they traveled the highways and many miles across many state lines making friends in the bluegrass world.

They were both loved by many, as they spent nearly all their 65 years together side by side.

Their life together is a constant reminder to us kids how much they loved each other.

A remarkable and blessed life they enjoyed.

Visit YouTube channel under
Donna Stacy to view videos,
please subscribe to the channel and like the videos